THE SI

Teresa Baldwinson

First edition published in Great Britain in 2013 by
TBR Consulting

Copyright © Teresa Baldwinson 2013

Teresa Baldwinson asserts the moral right to be identified
as the author of this work under the
Copyright, Designs and Patents Act 1988.

ISBN 978-0-9572606-8-9

TBR Consulting, Manchester M33 7EG, UK

Printed and bound by CPI Group (UK) Ltd, Croydon, CR0 4YY

Prologue

The Vatican had been a huge political force and a major player within the countries of Christendom before the Reformation. It still remained quite powerful afterwards too. Although in some countries the church's influence had then been lessened, it was strengthened in those states opposing its enemies. It was not often a matter of faith or morals, more of politics and the dirty in-fighting that can become. Truth, claimed as the first casualty of war, is also that of politics, a form of warfare fought with words not swords. Yet, even in that which had become mostly a hot-bed of intrigue, gossip and malevolence although within a pretence of piety, there were always many good, often hard-working people to be found. There is a saying that the cream always rises to the top. Unfortunately the scum frequently gets there first, being willing to climb on the faces of the rest.

This sequel is dedicated to those who were not the scum but who, having taken a vow of obedience, often had to be complicit even in evil. If their hands had not actually been tied, their tongues so often in effect were. In any judgements they often paid the price of the sins of the others. Whistleblowers have never had easy lives; when it also could have been said of them that they had broken their vow of obedience, their lives could be harder still. As Christ had been so hated by the powers-that-were in his time when he drove the money-changers out of the temple for robbing the poor, short-changing them beyond belief, so is the fate of anyone who stands in the way of illicit pleasures or wealth at the expense of others, especially when those others have a position of power.

Chapter 1

The burgeoning Renaissance which, with the Reformation, had given rise to calls for a counter-reformation by the Council of Trent. This had been seen to have extra unwished-for roots in the Vatican. On a bed of unrest the Florentine writer and philosopher, Machiavelli, published THE PRINCE. He put forward devious ways to rule effectively and safely whilst also governing autocratically. The ecclesiastical politicians making up the hierarchy, just like any of the other politicians of the day, were horrified to find some of their worst activities put before the literate public in this way. The civil authorities banished Machiavelli to a remote village and the Vatican said his books were not to be read, they were ceremoniously to be burnt. True to human nature, the literati avidly sought copies out to pass around. Reginald Pole was already among those at the Vatican seeking a fresh look and a positive renewal. Since the arrival of THE PRINCE such voices could then no longer be silenced. Rome has a rule by which it can review church teaching or behaviour which is seriously questioned by the educated faithful; it calls together a Vatican council. One of these was the Council of Trent where Pole chaired some meetings.

Cardinal Reginald Pole had never been finally ordained as a priest. A cousin of Henry VIII, they had originally been bosom friends. The Pole family had as good, if not better, claims to the throne than the Tudors. Yet, though twelve years into his reign Henry had the

Duke of Buckingham executed since he, too, could be a viable contender for the throne, Reginald still remained in friendship. When eventually Henry was seeking a divorce, Reginald had agreed with it as Pope Clement VII was originally happy to grant the request. That was until he realized it might have troops besieging the Vatican as that divorce affected the aunt of the powerful Charles V, the Holy Roman Emperor, the Duke of Burgundy, ruler both of Spain and the Netherlands. So the terrified Pope hastily revoked the case to the Vatican Curia. At that point, Reginald sided with the Pope, refusing the archbishopric of York. Going to Italy in 1532 he formed intimate friendships with many eminent men then eager for the internal reformation of the church, then an exceedingly corrupt institution. In 1535 he entered into a political correspondence with Charles V and was compelled by Henry to declare himself. He did this in a violent letter to the king, later expanded into the treatise, *"Pro Unitatis Ecclisiasticae Defensione"*. From then on Henry set a price on his head, and the remaining members of the Pole family - except Reginald who engineered to stay firmly out of Henry's reach - were systematically eliminated.

Though eventually a cardinal, Reginald had still only been ordained as a deacon. Instructed with Henry whilst Prince Arthur still lived and Henry had been destined for the church, their progress stopped before priesthood. But Pole had still been appointed bishop when in favour. Even though he was not a priest, Paul III made him into a cardinal in 1536, the position of a senior clerical administrator, and sent him to the Netherlands to confer with English malcontents there. Pole made several attempts to procure the invasion of England but with no success. In 1541-42 he was governor of the "Patrimony of St Peter" and was well-known as being fully in favour of a counter-reformation, clearing up the many bad practices that had become endemic. In 1545 he was a president of the Council of Trent and. by 1549. on the point of being elected pope. After he had failed to secure it with the election, instead, of Pope Julius III, he lived in retirement until the death of Edward VI when the ascendancy to the throne of England was in some doubt.

Ignoring the law of primogeniture, Henry's will had excluded the entire Stuart line of his elder sister, Margaret of Scotland, in favour of his younger sister, Mary Rose Tudor, grandmother of Lady Jane Grey and her younger sisters, Katherine and Mary. Further, He had also issued a statute which allowed the monarch to name his successor, a role constitutionally attributed to God's decision whereby who was to be first born. Edward took advantage of this statute by cutting his half-sisters, who had both been declared to be bastards, out of his will, bequeathing the throne instead to Lady Jane Grey Ascending to kingship as a minor, he had been strictly governed by his guardian, John Dudley, Duke of Northumberland, an exceedingly fervent Protestant and so he professed his own faith accordingly. Further, as both of his sisters were then unmarried he feared that, wed to foreigners, England might become an adjunct of a foreign empire. Also Mary Tudor was a Catholic.

Most Protestants were behind him in his wish,

especially those who were dismayed by the thought of a female rule running against their notions of traditional hierarchy and (according to some) biblical teaching. Lady Jane Grey and her sister Katherine were both Protestants, female, true, but married to Protestant Englishmen. It was no secret that Jane, merely sixteen years old, had been married against her will to Guildford Dudley, fourth son of that same Duke of Northumberland, Edward's guardian. She had even turned round and walked out of the room away from her new husband without a word to him. Her younger sister Katherine was wed to Henry Herbert, the Earl of Pembroke's son, both girls marrying on the same day.

However it was not only Catholics who preferred Mary Tudor; the Dudley family was well out of favour with many of the people. They were seen as being an ambitious, proud and ruthless clan. Taking advantage of the hatred and envy that the Dudleys inspired, when her brother died Mary, supported by very many ordinary people, overthrew Lady Jane Grey a mere nine days since she had been proclaimed queen. Though Mary was inclined to be lenient with the child, knowing as she did the problem was none of Jane's doing, when her father, the Duke of Suffolk, joined with Wyatt leading the Kentish men in support of her claim to the throne, she was executed as was also her husband and father-in-law. Pembroke, badly alarmed, took frantic steps to distance his family, having the as-yet-unconsummated marriage of his son to Lady Jane's sister, Katherine, immediately and openly annulled.

Since the monarch was expected not only to govern the realm but also to defend the kingdom, leading troops into battle when necessary and, though leaders were not often in danger of death in a battle, they would be more liable to be captured to hold for ransom. Queens, seen to be frailer, would then be more likely to cost their country more. There were also thought to be other practical reasons causing that reluctance to have a female at their helm. Would her feminine cycle interfere in matters of state. Moreover, though England had no Salic law forbidding such, those who could read might know of the bitter civil war that raged when the Empress Matilda, daughter of Henry I, fought for the crown against Stephen, grandson of William the Conqueror. Although it had happened many years earlier, even the unlettered could hear tell of it being repeated, especially since the later War of the Roses had so fiercely riven the country before the Tudor reign brought the peace with the white and red roses combined. So Mary's reign was never going to be an easy ride for her; it was made even riskier since her marriage to Philip of Spain, a ruler who, in the Netherlands, showed himself willing to walk roughshod over their ancient laws to export the hated Spanish Inquisition to their shores causing war in the Netherlands.

With Mary then as queen, Reginald Pole came back to England and out of retirement, hoping to fulfil his dream of bringing England back to a Catholicism as newly cleansed as possible, for which refurbishing he and others had been striving for some time. He was then commissioned to Queen Mary as legate "*a latere.*" As he was not a priest but still only in deacon's orders, Pole at first cherished the idea of marrying the queen. However, since Charles V had carried the match with his son Philip, he still remained to help Mary. Connected to royalty by birth, in his hopes and aims Reginald Pole carried few of the hallmarks of the meek who will in time - we are assured - inherit the earth, but at least he seems to have fully acknowledged the damages incurred by such overwhelming pride that would sulk after any reversals to hopes.

Arriving in London in 1554 with powers to allow the owners of confiscated church property the right to retain those possessions, he absolved parliament and country from schism and reconciled the Church of England to Rome. As long as Cranmer lived, Pole would not accept the Archbishopric of Canterbury Ordained priest in 1556, he eventually agreed to become its Archbishop after Cranmer was burnt much later. Pope Paul IV, irate at the concessions made by the authority of his predecessor to holders of former church property, revived accusations of heresy once brought against Pole. The Pope, also, was then at war with Spain and could not tolerate Pole as his ambassador at the court of Mary who was now the wife of Philip of Spain. (Footnote: The Vatican, a major political force was behaving accordingly.) So Pole's legation was cancelled and he was summoned before the Inquisition. When Mary protested, the Pope did relent but still would not reinstate Pole. Queen Mary, though like her father attending daily Mass and strongly professing Catholicism, still did not state her acceptance of full papal ruling by restoring annates to Rome that was still set against her husband's country.

It could be disputed how far Pole might have been responsible for Mary's heavy-handed persecution of Protestants, certainly because he was her supreme adviser, for the Spittalfield fires did not decrease in violence on any known insistence from him. Nor was a woman's pregnancy - as it had been in her father's day even for lesser punishments - a means of sparing any mother from the flames. Although many would claim that casual attitude to the sanctity of life to be part and parcel of the age then, there were contemporaries in positions of power who personally bucked that trend. William the Silent, *protege* of Charles V, during a session of 1564, defended the individual's rights even when they could be deemed to undermine the king's authority with these words, "However strongly I am myself a Catholic I cannot approve of princes attempting to rule the conscience of their subjects." Hearing this, Viglius van Aytta, an efficient civil servant representing Philip of Spain, spent a totally sleepless night worrying so much he had a stroke. Henri IV of France, also within the sixteenth century, though a decided libertine in his personal life, when bitter religious wars had riven the Continent, took the welfare of his subjects very seriously too when, as a Huguenot himself, to save unnecessary turmoil in the capital with the death rate it would bring, he attended a Catholic service saying, "Paris is worth a Mass." He is also reported as stating, "I want there to be no peasant in my kingdom so poor that he cannot have a chicken in his pot every

Sunday."

The great difficulty to be more humane arose because it was thought that God's anointed monarch ruled by divine right and that to differ from the views he or she held was therefore high treason not just against a ruler but against God Himself. Therefore the law proclaimed the death penalty for it. Such monarchs, then, had absolute power which so frequently corrupted absolutely. However, though power can corrupt and whilst human peers and their laws may exert their influence, it is still a fact that there have always been those few. Even with power, who could have had ideals not simply formed in someone else's jelly-mould. They appear to have noted that brains are God-given to use well with a touch more humanity than their peers may be showing at the time. A finely-tuned conscience is always required as well as that basic understanding of others' needs. Further, though a death penalty may then have been mandatory to some by laws they had not strictly observed, exceptional cruelty was not. Throughout the centuries, there have been some outstandingly shining examples of people who have tried to order their lives in such a way that would better bring about the common good as far as would be possible in their lifetime. Sadly, however, there were never as many of them as of those who would simply follow accepted, though hideously cruel, ways, never thinking it might matter.

The reason behind the idea of burning alive those adjudged to be heretics had always been stated to be in accordance with the scriptures, from Paul's first epistle to the Corinthians which declared, about those seen to be in the wrong, "Yet some may be saved yet so as by fire". Also, the hearts of both Mary and Reginald Pole could well have been hardened, each being very badly affected personally by their previous experiences, the Queen by the way her mother had been treated and she had been publicly bastardized, subsequently having to tread for most of her life on eggshells lest she, too, be executed, the Cardinal by his prolonged exile even whilst everyone of his immediate family - even his aged mother - would so summarily have been put to death That treatment may well have turned any would-be good heart to the very hardest stone.

The Queen and Cardinal Pole worked very closely and harmoniously together. Yet when, in one of her letters to him, she referred to her father Henry as being a good and pious man, Reginald rebuked her, pointing out various discrepancies in that opinion but applauding her filial love. However when, in 1558, he became dangerously ill, their lives were so totally intertwined that the Cardinal did actually die on the very same day as the Queen.

The burgeoning Renaissance is still visible within the Vatican itself. As its First Council, convened when the official teaching becomes out of synchronisation with the thinking faithful, Trent was partially to address the Church's claim that all outside this faith were said to be lost to God. The Renaissance was to challenge this view. Michelangelo, in his work on the Sistine Chapel from 1508 to 1512, portrayed the alternating presence of Prophets and Sybils, the seers of classic times, showing that he thought the hope of salvation lies outside of religious belief and involves the whole of mankind from its very inception.

Chapter 2

Local Work Continues

During Edward's reign the priest Harry had kept a much lower profile than before in their trading. He did not, however, think it proper totally to abandon the job which had brought welfare and food together with employment to the area. Instead he had introduced a young cousin, a young man named John, as driver. Mary Clare still accompanied John together with Bess, Alice's younger daughter and therefore Richard's niece. Her older sister Monica had started on her own career, promising to continue the work of her uncle. They might not have had so many of Richard's talents, but by their observations of what he had done and through their natural friendliness they were holding their own, helping their neighbours with their work.

Although nowhere near as inspired as her uncle had often been, Monica, by her diligence, her humility in seeking the advice of those nuns who had worked in accordance with Richard's teaching, was able to make the work progress still further. Bess, a bright and ever-cheerful girl, though forever joking and appearing scatter-brained, had a sharp, enquiring mind nevertheless. As a devoted follower of Isabelle, admiring the other girl so much that she appeared often almost to be her younger sister she was able, often, to wrong-foot many superficial opinions by sudden flashes of unexpected insight belying the notion of a naïve country girl simply following on the heels of someone she had loved.

Though it was slower than it had been under Richard and with his original lines still selling well, the range was noticeably and constantly being renewed by additions with nuances of other tastes or textures. One thing at which Monica excelled was that she kept notes of all the sales, which went well and where. Bess and John helped in this too, since neither had any pastoral work to cover also, as Harry's continuing pastoral role still did require him to do. Mary Clare, too, took her old duties very seriously concerning not only the welfare of the others who used to be nuns but also the children they had cared for in the convent. She had taken the advice of her predecessor whom they had called Auntie to ensure each child would be securely and happily lodged in the area. As all the children had been born and baptised within the parish bounds, there was help there for their care but, as Auntie had been sure to point out, care was not enough. They needed stability as youngsters but also the ability to become self-dependent and eventually dependable when older. As she had frequently insisted on remarking, "We may say we are bringing up children but this is not so: we are bringing up future adults."

In so many ways the ones engaged in Richard's work also helped in their own observations about their wares, all of which were reported back to Monica. So, though the range progressed, making additions, they found they could afford to sell the produce just a little more cheaply than before. With the increase in custom, they then had to buy in yet more milk from other farmers. Rather than taking too much from the nearby farms leaving the supplies there short for the local needs, on their ways back to base, John drove the cart round other farms, asking if they had milk to sell and at what price. The profits of their business in that way started to spread further as did also the liking for their produce once it had been tasted. It threatened to get rather too big for them to handle. So Harry, who had kept a watchful eye on this constant growth, stepped back in.

"I know I have always told you work makes work, and so it does, up to a point. But it does it better, and for longer, if with that work there is perceived to be good will. Do not in extending your growth neglect the herbal, curative arm of your work that you used to do. That is more easily perfected with people you know well for, though you may advocate a herb which would usually be a healer, people vary and some may find that that particular medicine is one which disagrees with them. It is truly a sensible thing to make a good living but you must define what you mean by "good". People may talk about the evils of greed and think they know the root of the problem but it goes more deeply and is subtler than that. If you have enough means to live, and just a little extra lest there may be an emergency, that constitutes a good life. Less than that and you will have to rely too much on yourself and that may stretch your abilities too far to live well. That can often be damaging to some. But a glut may be so much worse. You sometimes start to doubt your own abilities to survive if, by chance, any of that extra money were taken from you. That is when the means, instead of helping you in life, become the true ends in your life, the death of your essential being. Look, if you will, at our history. Before Constantine Christians were persecuted. They clung together, creeping quietly along, helping one another, keeping a low profile and hoping not to be killed by fighting nor eaten by wild animals for the pleasure of a crowd of out-of-work, rowdy Roman citizens. Then along came Constantine. It wasn't just that he became a Christian. Dante wrote it up in his INFERNO,

"Alas, Constantine, how much misfortune you caused, not by becoming Christian but by the dowry which the first rich father accepted from you."

"Which first rich father was that?" Mary Clare asked.

"Dear me," Harry said, "and you were a nun? It was Sylvester I, the first pope to become rich. After him, the Church became increasingly sold to money, so much so that when, much later, St Francis was ordered to rebuild the church when he was standing in the ruins of San Damiano's, he believed it to mean simply to rebuild that particular building. Which he did with his own hands. But the instruction in reality was to cleanse the whole Church of its dependence on money, to turn it back to its original reliance on God alone. He tried to do it, and everybody agreed with what he said - when he was there. But as soon as he had turned his back most seemed to revert to their previous customs. Even his own friends too. He specifically gave instructions that, on his death, he must be buried naked, not to waste the cloth of his habit, and no expense to be incurred for a tombstone to be erected there either. Yet, within two years, they had built a huge basilica over him in Assisi." Harry slowly shook his head.

"Well, this council, the one of Trent, will change all that, won't it" Mary Clare asked.

"It was supposed to do so," Harry told her, "and, to a point, so it will. Too many people, though, have become set in the old ways, especially those who had been in power and certainly do not wish to relinquish any of it; they would much prefer to stick with the status quo. But ordinary people too, some use the old customs of the Church as a child would look for comfort in his mother's arms. The Council of Trent was always going to go on and on for some time, especially because, though it had, true, some sincere advocates for renewal, as I said there were also those many who insisted on arguing against every point raised, who would truly have preferred everything to remain as it had been before. And they were supported by so many people who simply did not like any change. That is only to be expected when you think of it. However none of us, as yet, has had such huge power, or the immediate chance of getting it and we have all had seriously uprooting changes within our lives. But no matter what the final outcome at that level may prove to be, within our own selves and our spheres we, too, may have to judge for ourselves how we should best use some of those powers which we might actually be given."

"Oh my," Bess groaned but smiling as she did so, "you may not have been working as a parish priest lately but you still do preach as one."

Harry laughed, but with some sadness inherent in it.

"Whenever I look at you or think of you I am so reminded of Isabelle. I know you two were so often together but, fortunately for you, at this moment we can speak far more freely than was the case then. But beware; such was the charm of Isabelle's gaiety that it led to her death. Had we been less pleased with her winning ways we might have been harsher in our criticism of her talk and could have prevented her from becoming the victim of her tongue."

"So you think I have charming gaiety and winning ways, do you? " Bess said with an impish grin.

"Sometimes. Especially when they are unconsciously done. Not when you are simply fishing for compliments. Like now." Harry was laughing more freely. Bess, with her merry eyes and somewhat wayward hair on which she always found it hard to keep her cap, had her own ways of always lightening every conversation going but it didn't stop her from going back to any point she thought to be relevant or of importance.

"But about the new farmers we have bought milk from, do we have to tell them now that we don't want it? And have we to put our prices back up again as well?" she said. She was an intensely practical girl, as shown by the notes she, too, passed on back to her sister. Little details like how much difference the Counter-Reformation achieved or not meant less to her than how the cheeses, butters and relishes fared, how much money came in and what fraction of that, eventually, would be available to cover their needs. Further, in those notes she had also carefully entered any observation of a bad reaction that had happened from any herbs she had given and to whom it had occurred.

"No and no. But it would be as wise not to look for any more. Just be satisfied at the level - and the costs - we're at now. We are making a comfortable living as we are. Let us be satisfied with it. We cover the cheeses and the butters - from fruit as well as the ones milk-based - and the vegetable sauces which Richard started. Monica is working well on new lines; we will not be exactly standing still which usually means stagnating. In any case, going around to ever new farms further afield, when will there be enough time to do the actual selling"

They realised the sense of what he said but it was Bess who suggested how they could best take it further to proper ends.

"Mary Clare," she said, "are there any of your ex-nuns who are not so well employed just now? Some, maybe, needing something more worthwhile to do."

"I don't know of any but I'll ask. There may be one or two who don't feel the work they are doing is much more than a time-filler. Why?"

"Well, if there were others driving round, looking further afield for more milk but also showing our products, the sales could be rising along with any income and even more people can be given more work. That can't be a bad thing, can it?" Bess looked quizzically at Harry.

"You could have something there," he said, after a short pause. "I could perhaps find a decent ex-monk to accompany them if you wish. At least one on each cart well versed in the herbs too. The work that was started here has done very well for general well-being as well as our local economy. Spreading it further abroad could be a godsend to others too." He looked at Bess, beaming with approval. "Well done you for suggesting it."

"Thank you. But it's not done yet. We'll have to see how it works, and if it will work, before we celebrate."

Mary Clare was very quiet. In her mind she was going over all the names, and present jobs, of those who had been her nuns. She had a quiet smile on her face. At least two of them, very capable ones too, had been quite discontented. They had not felt they were truly gainfully employed; their employer appeared to believe they were tender flowers and so he did all the hard or heavy jobs, the ones most interesting or taxing. They were totally bored; each day seemed to drag along, but they were too polite to say so. They would jump at the prospect of really making a difference. She would put it to the employer as if he were doing the whole area an immense favour, which he could be doing, but impress on him that the ladies would be properly accompanied. She had learned from Auntie, a mistress of tact.

"We could spread it further," Bess said. "All right, we ask the farmers if they have enough milk to sell us. But for the fruits or vegetables we could ask the villagers if they, themselves, are growing or collecting any and if they have some to spare. It will spread more work and they too will have more money than they have now. And if we divide the work done so that milk products and those other kinds were made by different people they will not only be working faster but be specializing. Monica has worked on new lines but I'm sure she would be very pleased to see even more added when the new specialists get under way. And it will then give her more time to oversee all the reactions that we pass back to her...."

"Whoa back a little." Harry interrupted her flow. "They're all good ideas but we will have to develop them one by one. We can't get people excited by good prospects unless we have enough people *ready-trained* to deliver them. We have first to fulfil the present orders before we expand."

"So, when we go to the farms we are going to get more milk from, we could invite one or two of their older children to come and see our work. If we are giving the farmers top money for the milk we buy they will naturally be interested in the eventual products."

"Then they might want to make it for themselves," Mary Clare put in.

"So if they do, why not let them? If it furthers their well-being and that of their neighbours, what harm is there in that?"

"Bess I really do believe that, as long as you live and in the way you work, Isabelle will never be dead." Harry felt he could not have stated the case for expanding without being totally self-serving any better than she had.

Mary Clare, remembering Isabelle's lively concern for others, happily agreed.

Chapter 3

AND SPREADS FURTHER

Bess's idea worked very well. At first another three covered the area from north to west measuring from base, whilst John, Mary Clare and Bess travelled south to east. Seeing the way the locals' needs were now being better covered and all the wares they could make were selling well, the six talked to the farmers, inviting their older children to visit Monica and see the products made, to learn , too, about some herbs which, though sometimes very helpful, must be used first in small doses just in case they might not agree with the recipient. One or two of those children did indeed attempt to make cheeses themselves and sometimes ran into a little trouble. Bess, then, would call round to see if she could help in any way. The cheeses made from milk were, as Richard's had been, mostly either from goats or sheep. Monica developed them further with still the milk from all the different species having been kept separate. The customers commented on this, usually professing a special preference. These, too, were noted.

As others, having visited the place and seen how the wares were produced, began to make their own, sometimes with a slight moderation here or there, the locality became, at first merely mentioned, then known and eventually famous for its produce. The first hiccup had been when some people on one of the rounds had wished they were getting what another round was carrying.

Bess, once again, stepped in.

"If, say, once or twice a month, one member from each round would meet Monica to tell her what other things the people on his or her round would like, we could all be selling some of each other's stuff as well whilst some of our own was being sold by others."

"Do you think that would really work?" John, who should have been called Doubting Thomas, asked. "Would anyone give away any cheeses or pickles just because those selling from another cart wanted them?" A man who had just entered the novitiate once, John had previously had a tonsure. Of late his hair, on the patch that had been shaved, stood up like the bristles on a brush whilst that which had been the fringe hung lankly down, often getting in his eyes. It made him look like a simpleton but, in reality, although he tended to question everything, wanting to know all the details, he sometimes did point out fallacies others had simply either overlooked or ignored.

"Put like that," Bess said, "no. But Monica for us, another person for them, could check all our sales and give or take costs accordingly."

"Humm" was all John said. But in that one-syllable noise he had voiced his own disquiet, even suspicion at the prospect. He deeply doubted fragile nature, believing it to be neither overflowing with the milk of human kindness nor that unerringly accurate in accounting. His time in the friary, though very short, had also taught him that people, confined closely together, can make for a pecking order that is by no means governed by holy love.

However he seemed proved wrong. Guided still by Harry, not only were they soon working well in harmony but they were also carrying other things the villagers had made, with another level put under each cart to keep shoes, cloth or yarns etc. apart from the foodstuffs. With the monies the makers were given from the goods that were sold, and that which was given to those gathering vegetables or fruit for the sauces or fruit butters, that corner of the country was economically thriving. As - insisted on by Harry - the healing side of the trade, the herbs that would either cure or alleviate a sickness, or simply make a dish more attractive for a sick person to stimulate the appetite, was still an integral part of their rounds, what might otherwise have made for rivalry and jealousy turned, instead, into cooperation and further learning. For Harry had found that some of the newer carts had no herbalists on board. He had watched carefully, talked to people in the whole area ("Like the Presence of God," Bess said, "all over the place at once.") and he had found enough decent ex-monks not only to accompany every voyage of wares travelling but also to help plug the gaps in any knowledge of and training in healing. In their care for their customers' welfare they grew, though patchily at times, in the way they viewed each other ever more kindly. The area was becoming friendlier as it waxed, not hugely wealthy, but contentedly funded. Any money they made, too, they had happily worked for it. They helped each other without envy, progressing with no problems dictated by the thought of whoever would be on the throne. As Harry pointed out to them, now the pendulum of change had swung, further swings were sure to happen as night will follow day,

Chapter 4

THE BACKGROUND AROUND THE COUNTRY

Predominantly, Elizabeth (born 1533) showed her total belief in the right of primogeniture, that God had thereby demonstrated to whom He had given the divine right to reign. Though Mary Queen of Scots (born 1542) was thought to be her logical successor, Katherine Grey (born 1540) would thus have taken precedence but for her father's execution for treason excluding her personally from the Throne. To Elizabeth's mind, Katherine would otherwise have been her rightful heir.

In the last months of Mary's reign Katherine was a maid of the Privy Council. Across the country thousands were dying from influenza and some of the queen's ladies were ill. Katherine's friend, Jane Seymour, the niece of Henry's third wife, succumbed to it and developed a fever. Katherine was given permission to leave to nurse her friend at the country home of the Duchess of Somerset, Jane's mother. Her 19-year-old brother Ned was also there and Katherine and he became good friends. The Duchess warned him; Mary was then very ill and any romance between him and Katherine could make a dispute as to Elizabeth's succession as Jane's marriage had made for Mary. But love is not the only one blind; friendship can be deaf as well.

When Mary Tudor died one of Elizabeth's first actions was to demote Katherine as a maid of the Privy Council to the Presence Chamber which sent out a clear message that whoever wished to gain Elizabeth's favour must beware of becoming too friendly with Katherine. But that first summer, before Elizabeth had acquired her full perceptions of her new position, she was too busy pursuing her own passion for Robert Dudley to be so vigilant about other things and a romance between Katherine and Ned Seymour was able to grow. The couple later remembered the royal progress of 1559 as the time they both fell completely and passionately into love during the summer banquets and garden walks. But it was Elizabeth's devotion to Dudley which was the subject of court gossip.

In 1560 many believed Elizabeth's affection for Robert, one of the hated Dudley clan, would lead to her overthrow. Ambassadors and privy councillors discussed the arrangements of a suitable marriage for Katherine, as her heir. The Spanish hoped to see her marry a Hapsburg, strengthening the English-Spanish ties. Elizabeth's councillors spoke instead of the Earl of Arran, heir to Mary Queen of Scots and leader of the Scottish Protestants. Meanwhile Katherine secretly had already pledged herself to marry Hertford, a promise made with "kissing, embracing and joining their hands together" in his sister's private closet at Whitehall Palace. Also Edward Seymour, Earl of Hertford, for all his youth and lack of experience, was exceedingly well-connected. Another descendant of Edward 111, he was also the nephew of Jane Seymour, mother to Edward Vl.

Sir William Cecil, Katherine's kinsman, had started his career in the household of Hertford's father and had risen to become Elizabeth's secretary of state. He was among those most concerned about her devotion to Robert Dudley. In 1560 on 6 September he told the Spanish ambassador that he "clearly foresaw the ruin of the realm through Lord Robert's intimacy with the Queen". He actually wished Dudley dead twice. But that same evening Dudley's wife, Amy Robsart, was the one to die. Her corpse was found at the foot of a short flight of stairs in the house of one of her friends. The coroner's jury returned a verdict of death by misadventure. There was a suggestion of suicide. The more popular conclusion, however, was that Dudley had killed his wife. Cecil's great fear was that Elizabeth would marry Dudley despite the common wave of revulsion for him. But the queen made it plain that she understood this to be impossible, It does appear as if, at this point, she realized she could only reign not solely by divine right but also by the will and with the consent of her people.

Hertford's and Katherine's liaison, however, did continue. Cecil advised the lad to pull back and he dutifully stopped his courtship of her, even flirting with another girl at court. But Katherine wrote him a furious letter and, fearing he might lose her completely, their nuptials were brought forward. They married in December 1560 with only his sister Jane as witness, in his bedroom in a house on the Thames. After a brief toasting of the marriage, Jane withdrew and they went to bed to make love with Katherine naked except for her fashionable headdress. They arose at one point, then went back to bed again to make love once more before hurrying back to court before they could be missed.

During that late winter to early spring they met for passionate moments in many of the Queen's palaces as well as Hertford's London house. In March his 19-year-old sister, Jane, died. In the same month Katherine began to suspect she might be pregnant but, scared of its implications, convinced herself she must be mistaken. Since Hertford was eager to go on a trip to Europe she ignored the signs and assured him he ought to go. Cecil, knowing they were involved but unaware of the marriage and anxious to keep them apart, had explained to her that it was for their own good. Katherine was eight months pregnant and on another summer progress with the court before she told anyone else. Then she confessed to Robert Dudley and begged him to intercede for her with the Queen. He failed to mollify Elizabeth who feared another plot, such as the one which had led the sister Jane to the scaffold. She sent Katherine to the Tower. Recalled from Europe, Hertford was also imprisoned in the Tower, arriving there 5 September 1561. Elizabeth, suspecting this to be a ploy for the throne, did not know who might be involved. The Spanish ambassador thought Cecil to be behind the union, and Arundel's name also was mentioned. But the couple's testimony revealed no such reason behind the union, merely two headstrong youngsters with a huge, overwhelming passion for each other who had steadfastly ignored the wise advice others had given them.

Elizabeth had, at the same time, another contender for her throne. James Hepburn, Earl of Boswell, had travelled to France to persuade the widowed Mary to return to Scotland as the anointed Queen of Scots to lead the fight in her country in its struggles about its sovereignty. Although Mary had been born in 1542, later than Elizabeth in 1533, she nevertheless could have claimed right of primogeniture on the grounds that her grandmother, Margaret, Henry's older sister, had the prior claim when the male heir, Edward VI, died. Scotland fought England for this right but had lost. Mary had then refused to ratify the peace treaty that demanded she now recognize Elizabeth as queen. On 8 September William Maitland, Mary's adviser, came to Elizabeth in the castle of Hertford with letters from Mary. She would agree to sign the treaty, but only if Elizabeth would name her as heir not Katherine Grey. With all her troubles, Maitland found the queen, "extremely thin and the colour of a corpse". Though Mary's letters offered affection to her cousin, the ones from other members of the Scottish nobility were very much harsher. For all that Elizabeth replied firmly that she had expected a very different answer than the one given, in the subsequent interview it became obvious that, a staunch Protestant herself, she did actually think Mary, though Catholic, would be more suited to the monarchy than the headstrong Protestant Katherine. But she was not inclined to meddle as it could provoke a debate in England that would affect Mary's interest. She said, "I here protest to you that I know no better, nor that I myself would prefer to her, or yet, to be plain with you, that case that might debar her from it." By that statement Elizabeth made it abundantly clear that she preferred the tradition of primogeniture to be more important than those decided by English statute and her father's and brother's wills. She appeared to understand what they had not; introducing new ways of appointing heirs interfered with any notion of the divine right for the monarch to rule since only God had chosen who would be born first. Elizabeth, speaking to Maitland about Katherine and the third Grey sister, Lady Mary, mentioned the 1554 revolt against Mary Tudor and claimed that they would be unable to inherit since their father had been executed along with Lady Jane Grey.

Though well-known as a Protestant queen, Elizabeth initially was fully aware of those of her courtiers who crept secretly to Masses celebrated daily in the Catholic embassies. There were undoubtedly noted martyrdoms within her reign but it was at a later stage and they were more often politically and locally motivated than had been the case under Mary whose Spanish husband not only had the Inquisition at home but, by attempting to put it into action in the Netherlands also, was disliked and reviled by many. Under Elizabeth, when spiteful neighbours might report people for having Masses said in their houses the law was set which action must ensue. As, to tell people there would be a Mass, the custom was to set a vase of hawthorn, preferably in blossom, in the window, it was easily done for any neighbour with a grievance to inform the authorities. Further, judges then had very little discretion and were held to account if they were deemed to be too lenient. So judges' lives were often seen then to be in jeopardy and always remarkably short, therefore they often made the most for their families' futures whilst they could. Anyone charged for what was a capital offence, having pleaded, could have any property confiscated, some of which could possibly stray into the judge's hands.

The Queen, however, although as brutal in many ways as her father had been, in the earlier half of her reign showed more leniency than others might have done. Probably from the revulsion she felt as a toddler when her mother was executed, she did not always look on capital punishment as being the only answer to any problem.

A further worry was added to Elizabeth when, on 24 September 1561 Katherine was delivered of a son, Edward Seymour, Viscount Beauchamp, yet another claimant for the throne. The baby at two days old was baptised in the church at the Tower a few feet from the decapitated remains of his aunt, Lady Jane Grey. Cecil, fearful of the possibilities following this birth, was urging Elizabeth to marry. She, having seen how little good had come to her sister Mary from her marriage, was unwilling to be forced up a bridal path for which she had no wish. Instead, she tried to discredit the validity of Katherine's marriage, ordering a church commission td do it. This might have proved easy; the sole witness, Hertford's sister, was dead and the priest could not be found. But the only necessities to make a marriage valid was a solemn declaration of intent followed by sexual intercourse. This had happened as they had stated in the interrogations of them since they had been imprisoned. But the problem was further aggravated since sympathetic warders were allowing Ned to creep quietly along the corridor to Katherine's room to allow them to lie together on her bed. Elizabeth, unaware of this security leak, was planning to meet Mary Queen of Scots in Nottingham to seal an alliance for the Stuart line to succeed her. This was, however, forestalled by a massacre of Protestants in France by followers of Mary's Guise uncles. Then, just as Elizabeth was getting her wish to declare Katherine's baby illegitimate, a second son was born to in February 1563.

Elizabeth, showing herself still unwilling to sign their death warrants, simply had the lieutenant of the Tower, Sir Edward Warner, locked up for his laxity within his own prison. The young couple were then separated in different country houses that were, effectively, their jails. From hers, Katherine wrote passionate letters to her "Ned", saying "I long to be merry with you," calling him, "My sweet bedfellow, that I once lay beside with joyful heart and shall again." Unfortunately for her, that never happened. In January 1568 her warder, Sir Owen Hopton, asked the royal doctor to help her, but she had no wish to live. Instead she begged Hopton to return her wedding ring to Hertford with a parting gift of another ring inscribed, "While I lived, yours." She died aged 28; Hertford, freed in 1571, survived her to be 84 having found, in his last years, the priest who had officiated at their marriage.

Meanwhile Elizabeth was still hopeful that Mary should succeed her. However, there was a law dating back to Edward III that anyone born outside the realm of England would be excluded from succession. John Hales, an MP and friend of William Cecil, wrote a book attacking Mary's claim and quoting that law. Elizabeth was furious about his "writing so precisely against the Queen of Scotland's title" and sent Hales to the Tower. But so many senior figures were involved, she had to overlook their actions. She desperately wanted to be able to trust Mary. So she offered her own love, Robert Dudley, as husband to Mary, giving to him the title Earl of Leicester to make him more attractive. Instead Mary married Lord Darnley, another grandchild of Margaret Tudor. When their son James was born, Cecil and Walsingham redoubled their efforts to have Mary excluded from the throne. New tracts were published and, in October 1556 the MPs supporting Katherine brawled on the floor of the Commons, fighting for the right to debate the succession against the queen's command. Petitions followed but Elizabeth steadfastly refused to name any heir. However Mary, shooting herself in the foot, destroyed any hopes she might have had when Darnley was murdered and she married the Earl of Boswell, the man who had induced her to return to Scotland but, more tellingly, the man who was believed to have killed her husband. Mary was forced to abdicate; Scotland had rejected her and crowned her 13-month-old son James as king in her stead. He, then, continued that long history of the Scottish monarchy coming to the throne as babes or young children, the country being mal-administered meanwhile with many powerful and unfriendly magnates who simply jockeyed for their own ends, ignoring any public or national welfare.

Mary fled to England but Elizabeth had neither the

will to execute her, as she was advised to do, nor the graciousness to let her go. She imprisoned her, eventually in Fotheringhay Castle. Mary and her fervent adherents continued to show an amazing amount of foolishness in pursuing her right to rule. The fact that Scotland, the land where she had truly been their anointed Queen, had effectively disowned her, did not give them any hint that, had she been Queen of England, it would never have been accepted quietly and without a vicious civil war ensuing. Nor did they notice that, at that time, it was not only Protestants who would prefer they did not succeed, many Catholics also wanted to continue the comparatively more peaceful life they had then.

So then there came a succession of plots that were not only of no avail but also not kept secret enough. The Babington plot was the culmination when they planned to kill Elizabeth and have Mary crowned as queen. After that the penal times came in with a vengeance for Catholics. It was treason for a priest to be in England and a felony to harbour one. In the country, however, there were many well-born Catholic families who had withstood an interdict in the past, when priests had been forbidden to say Mass or minister all sacraments except for the baptism of infants and extreme unction for the dying. Such families had chapels and private chaplains who simply and quietly went about their normal duties, the excommunication of a king and any interdict notwithstanding. Many of them had chosen to rearrange their wainscoting to conceal a roomy cupboard where, if necessary, the priest and his accoutrement could be able to take refuge if the house were searched.

Elizabeth, then, could no longer refuse to sign Mary's death warrant. She had delayed too long, fearing the possible result even to herself by having an anointed queen condemned to death. Cecil and Walsingham had been strongly advising she did exactly that beforehand but, after such a plot which had been both bolder and more thorough than the rest, as noted critics of Mary, they redoubled their cries to have an end put to such a danger. For, though she relied heavily on both of them - Cecil as her chief secretary of state and, for many years, the true architect of Elizabethan greatness, and Walsingham who, with Cecil, ran such a network of spies which had, for instance, uncovered the Babington plot - had Mary survived later to reign both men knew they would be immediately executed as her main adversaries.

There were some discrepancies, however, in the ways the penal laws were enforced. Cecil had been very keen on backing trade, making sure that its paths should be smoothed. Walsingham, too, was aware, for instance, that Shakespeare, related to the Catholic Ardens, was strongly rumoured to be a secret Catholic himself. But he had bought into The Globe to ensure his prosperity, and his plays were being very well received even by the Queen. Further, any criticism of the state he made in those plays he firmly set in other countries. So some blind eyes could be discreetly turned, when it was considered the occasion warranted it. Certainly keener eyes could have caused more trouble, less general progress in the land, had they wished to do so. They considered there were enough examples of martyrs to be found without any dire need to add more.

Such plotters like those involved with the Babington, however, had done no favours for Catholics in the land. Many of the priests, coming over from Douay to say Masses, who, when found and taken to execution had, as one of their final prayers, the desire for the welfare of Elizabeth and England. Margaret Clitherow, known as the Pearl of York, was in fact the Catholic wife of a Protestant butcher. They had a very happy marriage, helping one another; he claiming the only way by which his wife caused any trouble at all to him was by the fines he had to pay since she did not wish to attend the parish church services. When she was found harbouring a priest she was imprisoned for her trial. The warders knew her from the many times she had been there for her refusal to go to the local church. Initially she had been unable to read; like most women of her time, she had never been schooled in anything other than housewifely duties. She learned whilst in gaol, sometimes asking of any problems from the warders. They grew fond of her as a constantly cheerful and helpful prisoner. When any of them would be having troubles at home, a fretful wife, babies teething or older children giving grief, she would listen to such woes, giving advice if she could as from an older woman to a younger man. At other times she sang or simply chatted to and merrily joked with them, making their day's work less tiresome. At her trial she refused to plead, which was her right. By that way her trial may not proceed, her husband and children would not be forced to give testimony against her, nor could they subsequently be deprived of their goods and livelihood maybe, and, if turned out to the streets, not even given the normal help from the parish. The judgement then was that she be stripped and kept closely confined in a totally bare cell for three days, fed only on a diet of barley bread and puddle water. This would give her a form of dysentery and, with male warders, maybe break down her resistance with her feeling of shame. After those three days, if she still refused to plead, she was to be laid on that dirty floor with a sharp stone to press into her spine and be covered by a plank of wood. The warders then had to put other small stones on the wood to press her very slowly to death in the hopes that she would finally yield and submit a plea. Such was their respect and affection for her, however, they chose instead to use the biggest stones there, to throw them hard so that her agony might not be so prolonged. There were many in York, Catholics or Protestants, who knew her as a very good neighbour. They were such who then named her as The Pearl of York, a play on words since the name Pearl is a variation of Margaret.

Chapter 5

PROBLEMS OCCUR

Harry had been severely ill and was advised to retire. But total retirement was never on his schedule. Though for some time he no longer had taken part in the actual trading, he was always prepared to advise, sometimes more frequently and more verbosely than they might have preferred, although he often made good points from which they benefited. How he learned exactly what was happening to them at any time did amaze them. The gossips, they reckoned, must be keeping him up-to-date. It was at such times that he wrote letters, applauding their work initially, then criticizing, advising and cajoling their efforts. It was for one such incident that he stepped in when it looked, for all the world, as if their work could be in danger of falling apart.

A new person had started on one of the other routes. David, an ex-monk, still on a pension from the time he had been told he was too young, then, to become a friar, he was still older than either of the two women he accompanied. He was well-versed, true, in herbal usage but he came fresh to the local trade. Yet he was extremely sure any ideas of his were so much better than theirs and, further, he was their senior. So, whenever he thought one thing when they knew how wrong his notions would be, he expected to overrule them The two ladies fumed at this, and not so silently too. Some others took sides, then there were those in the middle who told all their colleagues they just did not want to know. That cooperation they had once known was now thoroughly fractured, almost beyond repair.

Harry wrote to Monica, knowing full well she would read out his advice to the rest. First he praised them for appointing a new person with such a good working knowledge of herbs, reminding them that many people, since the monasteries and the hostels they previously kept had been sold to private owners, were now without their previous health advisers. Then he pointed out that we can all get just as set in our ways as we may be in our joints when we age. We would be needing adjustments on all sides, to use all benefits, with due praise, to the full, and to explain what else is to be done and why. He told a story.

"There is a Carmelite nun now, Teresa, who obtained permission to bring back the ancient and stricter rule of Carmel to a small house in a place called Avila in Spain and now has been urged to extend her ideas to sister houses. She travels around, advising them, pleading with them, even ordering them at times. Many had fallen into the ways of easy living, some had almost sold their souls to luxury or money. She found them actually more willing than she expected to accept, even embrace, the lives she was holding out to them.

"One house, however, gave her more concern than the others. Though seemingly reasonable women, it was a hotbed of squabbles, factions fighting and re-forming, no one person appearing to agree with anyone else on any one topic or for very long. They were not evil people, they were simply without a fair share of holy love. Teresa was at her wit's end, not knowing how to tackle this problem. Then they got an infestation of fleas.

"Teresa ordered everyone to go to their cells, wash themselves thoroughly and put on fresh clothes, laundering the clothes they had worn and all their bed linen, scrubbing their cells out thoroughly. Then they had to carry on outside, scouring all of the passages also. That, she told them, would have to be done on a daily basis for some weeks until not only all the fleas were dead but the eggs also. At first, when they had finished in the cells, they joined in the work outside, squabbling as usual. Gradually, in conjunction against their common enemy that was the flea, they began to work together, first in a kind of truce, eventually in open cooperation. By the time they were rid of the infestation they were all members of a really friendly house.

"Then Teresa wrote a hymn, thanking the almighty God for giving them the fleas which had caused them to grow so much in love and help for one another. She had the newly-cooperative - and actually happier - nuns walking in procession around the chapel, smiling as they sang that hymn.

"I do not hope you may be blessed with an infestation of fleas but that you may note what Teresa found: that working together as harmoniously as possible not only gets the job done better but is so much more pleasant for all. If a new idea is put forward, don't summarily dismiss it; look at it seriously from all angles, discussing it with total courtesy but not patronisingly. Work together or sink separately, it is your choice."

True to Harry's belief, Monica read this letter out to each team as they came back to her, then, to remind all of it, to those who would be representing their teams when they came to a meeting together.

When she heard it, Bess laughed, then capered about, scratching her head and body, pretending she were bedevilled by fleas. The others were all as amused by that performance as they had been by the idea of Teresa writing that hymn. From then on, whenever a small dispute might look as if it were about to arise on the carts, it would be cut short with head-scratching and grins all round. The very idea of flea-infestations worked to unite them as much as it had for the quarrelsome Carmelite nuns about whom Harry had written.

Chapter 6

BESS IS CONFUSED

Bess had been mulling over everything she had heard from Harry. At the same time she had watched the penal times bite more stringently and believing, as she did, that they had arrived as the direct result of the plans to assassinate Elizabeth, she felt those plotters did no one any good. So, one day when she was back from her travels and had reported her sales and people's needs, along with the findings of any reactions to herbs, she made her way over to where Harry was living in his retirement.

"So why," she asked directly, "if your Council of Trent told everyone that - what was it you claimed? - *"the hope of salvation lies outside of religious belief and involves the whole of mankind"* do we still find that there are some Catholics busy trying to kill Elizabeth just because she was a Protestant queen? That Council was done with Vatican approval and was supposedly aimed to tell us how we should behave. It doesn't make sense at all to me."

"Nor to me," Harry admitted ruefully "But I also said, did I not, that those either in power or lusting for it are not likely to want to see any change coming in which might deprive them of it. To them religion is merely a name, a peg on which they can hang any cause through which they seek to rule others. True religion, as Christ taught us, is based on good relationships; love of God and care for your neighbours. Killing anyone for power simply does not come under that heading. Then, of course, there are those not looking for any supremacy but merely that they be allowed to survive and practise their own faith. I suspect their numbers are actually greater, but the power-hungry may be shouting more stridently, drowning out those who merely want to live and let live."

Bess was still less than convinced.

"But I don't hear anyone from the Vatican telling us that Trent advised us that we ought to seek good relations with others. Why doesn't it?"

"The Vatican", Harry pointed out, "was not totally in favour of calling a council. Why should it be? It is itself a political force and the damages of those politics are just as bad for it as they are for any other autocratic state. How many parents do you find letting their own children rule them? Those who sought a council were frequently judged to be heretics. Sticking your neck out for change when bosses feel very happy as they are, thank you very much, can be a simple recipe for losing your head."

"So why then did it call any council? It it's so very powerful, what caused it to let the whole thing happen?"

"Ah," Harry sighed, "there's the rub. When I said it is a political force I meant just that. It has Vatican states, embassies, all the trappings not only of its individual strength but also for the balance of power between nations. Politics is a cut-throat business. There is a saying that the cream always rises to the surface. When any individual is intent on his own gain, however, the scum will be very likely to get there first, being willing to contaminate as it rises. The Church, however, was promised Christ's help. And we can truly believe that His promises are signed and sealed, but they have never been dated. The Church, however, is more than only the Vatican. All who admit to having Christ at their head will be part and parcel of the Church. Further, we all, laity or clergy, in any religion or none, have a particular God-given vocation, I believe, in order to make this world work as well as it might. We are given gifts to help us and it is up to each one not to be stupid, thinking, "My parents weren't such-or-such therefore I could never become something I know I truly ought to become to help others". That is either false modesty or total snobbery, dependant on if you should be taking a higher rank or lower from the one your parents held. A calling is given to be fulfilled or you might even run the risk of upsetting God's plans for our world."

"My!" Bess said, her eyes round as saucers. "I never thought I'd hear a priest telling me I could upset the plans of God. We say "the Almighty God". If almighty, surely it means He can do whatever He likes, doesn't it?"

Harry laughed. "Of course. But since we've been given free will it must take longer to make a thoroughly good society that works harmoniously and happily together if we would refuse the gifts we've been given to us all to let it happen."

"Well, you believe this, but did the Vatican think, before Trent, that no other people counted too, that God had made us, but that all those outside our own circle were predestined to damnation?"

"Bess, Bess, Bess," Harry shook his head at her. "Talk of predestination is taking us into a whole new realm of ideas. One at a time is enough to handle, to do it well."

"Well *you* were the one who strayed from what Trent meant to the idea we all have vocations." Bess laughingly chided him.

"All right," he agreed. "You win. This time, that is. Just don't make a habit of it or I'd think you were aiming to become a priest."

Bess shook her head. "Not at all. If I were hoping for anything like that it would be to become a cardinal."

Harry grinned at her. "Reginald Pole could get there before being ordained as a priest but *he* wasn't female. It does count, you know."

"Yes," Bess admitted. "But those rules were made up by men, weren't they? Further, they were done when, as practising Jews, women in their fertile years might only be able to do those jobs three-quarters of the time. So men were chosen instead."

"Do you know," Harry said with a grimace, "I think I've taught you far too much and far too well. You're about outshining me, tying my arguments into knots against me."

Bess laughed. "I truly doubt I'd ever be able to do that. But, though I'm no longer in my first springtime myself, I might tire you out and wear you down. So…" she looked around. "Is there anything you want me to get you whilst I'm here, or to bring back next time I come?"

Harry shook his head. "No, but thank you for asking. There are two great-grandchildren of one of the ladies I used to visit; they keep me well supplied. But your presence is like a breath of fresh air to me. I feel younger for talking with you, not just like a silly old man who can't do anything for himself but is only sitting around waiting for God's call."

Bess blew out her cheeks. "Phew. Don't say that. Any time someone might think you silly, tell them to come see me. I'll put them right immediately. Anyway," she concluded, "it is high time I went back. The rest will think I've run away with some troubadour, or more likely with last week's takings. I'll be back to see you again. Stay well and with God."

They made their farewells then but Bess never did return to see him for, a few days later, he quietly died in his sleep.

Chapter 7

DIVISIONS? WHAT DIVISIONS?

Harry's funeral was a true eye-opener for any powers-that-be there. For a start, the local parish priest, a Protestant, approached Monica to ask her if he could have what he called "the privilege of officiating" at the burial. Then so many different people in the area were getting together, organizing food and drinks for whoever wished to attend. He had helped so many people in his lifetime, they, and sometimes their descendants, wanted to honour him in his death. As the pastor put it, "Even if he didn't think as I do, he was ever courteous, never judgemental, and forever willing to help if he could."

A local hotelier, a Protestant, came forward to offer his place for the reception whilst his wife, a Catholic, would be busy looking after those who would have to stay over if they had travelled very far. Further, the money he asked for that service was enough just to cover his costs and no more.

A nearby farmer, of a similarly mixed-rites family, said they would see all travellers' horses were properly groomed, fed and generally cared for whilst the owners attended the funeral.

A middle-aged lady, who professed no belief that anyone knew anything about but whose own mother had constantly been helped by Harry whilst she, herself, had learned much about herbs and nursing from him, came forward to say she would be honoured to give her services if required.

On the day itself all the discussion centred not on his religion nor on his role as a priest but rather on his care for other people.

One woman there was heard to remark, "I once heard him say that God made us all different, giving each one an individual's own talents and calling and, if God didn't make us the self-same beings, we should not be either so proud or so stupid as to believe we know better than He did, thinking that we should all be alike." The middle-aged lady of unknown faith nodded her head, but in her mind she substituted "nature" for the power of God. Privately she would have preferred to be able openly to call herself an atheist. That, however, might have either the wrath of or a discourse from both Catholics and Protestants alike descending on her head. Therefore she kept her own counsel quietly to herself. Harry had understood, she remembered.

Having got rid, in that way, of the metaphysical they then proceeded recounting the practical, the good the man had done, the work and the due prosperity he had helped to come to the area. For all that they had been fond of him, his funeral was fast turning into a celebration of his life rather than a mourning for his death. Bess alone, she felt, was truly missing him; he had been someone not only to turn to for advice but also to use, bouncing new ideas off him. She was bereft and silent in shock.

David, who had once threatened the workings of their trade but who had benefited very greatly since, apparently learning so much from Harry's ways and wisdom, noticed Bess's silence and went over to her.

"When people die, you know," he told her, "it is by no means the end of their time with you. What they told you, what they taught you, it's with you still, in your head. You may find yourself thinking *What would Harry say about this* and almost believe you hear his answer because you remember the very ways he thought and looked at things. No one is truly dead to this world whilst they're still remembered, whilst their example is living on."

Bess stared at him, this man who had come so close to breaking up their trading partnerships.

He continued unabashed. "All these people here know they have benefited from knowing him, that if they but continue along the same path he would have helped them on he will, in one way, be with them for as long as they live. Probably longer, if they pass it on to their children." He paused; Bess still stared, but less in wonder, more in growing thoughtfulness.

"I had a very good friend, my mentor," he was reminiscing, "I thought I could not have endured living in that community but for him. There were so many cliques, so much petty rivalry. Something like Teresa had found in that convent of hers. But I was just a newcomer; I felt left out of all friendships 'til James taught me not to be afraid, to be friendly and helpful to all and then to be willing to accept friendship from others. But he advised me not to join in gossip or backbiting; if someone finds fault with another don't argue; simply say something like "Perhaps he meant it well, he maybe just got it wrong somehow." James died; he was killed when our house was being closed. I felt not only lonely but lost. And when I joined this group and then, when Harry had written that letter to us, I went home to break down and cry like a baby. When I'd done, though, I heard in my head all that James had taught me and I almost felt as if he were by my side." He took a deep breath, obviously trying to control the tears that were threatening him. In a somewhat strangled voice he concluded, "Harry is your James, isn't he"

She nodded mutely, not trusting herself to speak. David patted her on her shoulder, nodded also and, unable to speak himself, quietly left her pondering on what he had said. She was still in silence, unusually absorbed, not at all her ebullient self. But she was, at least, no longer in shock. Others who had noticed made a mental note to thank David later for his kindness to Bess. Monica, especially, had been very worried by her sister's pallor and abnormal withdrawal. She was gratified to see more colour coming back to her sibling's cheeks. Breathing a huge sigh of relief, Monica knew Bess maybe would not like but could now weather the storm and whatever it would bring.

Chapter 8

RISING HOPES

Queen Elizabeth was fully showing her own acquired wisdom. Cecil may and did advise her but any final decisions were hers and hers alone. She had renounced any idea of marriage but, apart from Spain, she pretended otherwise and kept all the other countries in the air, hoping they could make an alliance through matrimony with her. She used the chivalry of her own subjects, sometimes as at Tilbury under a cloak of her own strength and determination, to fill the treasury of the country. More fine and fast ships were built and many sailors of note were commissioned to behave like pirates when meeting any Spanish galleons. When those ships were sailing back to Spain with gold and treasures seized from the New World, some from the English fleet would attack and board them to confiscate such wealth. Then, when Phillip sent an armada to sack England, Drake, one of her prize captains, defeated them before they could ever reach the shore. Spanish ships were burnt in their home port to "singe Phillip's beard". At home Elizabeth's standing grew as did her navy and, but for Spain, between all other countries kept still hoping for a matrimonial alliance with England, and the way that the Spanish were openly distrusted for denying the Netherlands her ancient treaties, the fame of the English abroad also rose in general with its good effect on trade and exports. Knowing this strength, at one point

William the Silent petitioned Elizabeth for help against the Spanish and, though there was never any formal aid given, Phillip was known to be exceptionally annoyed by the way the request was received with obvious sympathy for the plea.

But, though admired - even loved - by many, no one, least of all a monarch, has no enemies. Walsingham, cynically but in the circumstances wisely employing a bevy of spies, kept danger at bay or at least to the minimum. This was widely known and therefore, in fear of retribution, exceptionally few further plots matured to become any real danger. This led to Elizabeth receiving further admiration, each subject's feelings growing, echoing or reflecting that of others. But the damage this could wreak on the subjects themselves did not go away.

When other opinions then the ones generally held may be openly voiced they can and most probably will be disputed. If, however, they are kept artificially mute they often fester with deep resentment. Within small areas this can be lessened since the force of usual feelings may thereby be weakened by the fewer number of people there holding them and by the simple fact that it was often necessary to be able to rely on the goodwill of the neighbours to continue to survive. However, no matter how remote any area may be, perfect harmony is very highly unlikely to be there.

Though far from court, parliament and the back-biting that would be endemic there, in any hamlet however small there will almost always be some dissent. This may well not centre on who may be the person to inherit the throne, perhaps not even on any religious themes; it would more likely be about a local topic or for personal dislikes, petty rivalries or even sibling jealousies. They are very similar to problems found at court but maybe in a degree of miniature. Such may even become aggravated simply by the size of the place in someone who feels trapped and longs to be a fish in a larger pool than in his or her own home town. Someone usually young and wanting to meet more people than so far seen but always a person who is deeply discontented. Each village, hamlet or even family may be nurturing such a one as that.

The worm in the bud of that prosperous area where the trading had occurred was not a youngster but an adult shoemaker. He had been greedy and had used second-rate hide and sloppy work whilst charging full price for his wares, pocketing the difference and knowing full well new shoes would be needed very soon by the same person. That was when he had been the only shoemaker nearby and found no other shoes around which might compete with his. But when these traders put a stop to his ways by putting more than their foodstuffs on their carts, overnight he had lost his local monopoly of its foot-ware. He had been looking since for a way of stopping his enemies but knew full well that the benefits they brought to the tenor of life generally around him made it an almost impossible thing for him to achieve without also losing his own ability to function - and with that the extra profit he once had - among the local populace. So he had waited for an opportune moment, hoping such might one day happen, preferably quite soon too.

Then one Sunday at church he heard the parish pastor who had officiated at Harry's funeral quoting a quip which he said came from THE PRINCE. This was a book which had been proscribed by the Vatican which, by no means always getting things right on matters that were especially not of faith or morals, was notoriously late in saying, "Oops, sorry, we got that wrong." Its habit was rather to lay low, letting people almost forget its previous stance, hoping all would blow over. But THE PRINCE was not just about the ways of the Vatican; what Machiavelli wrote covered all secular rulers also. The shoemaker looked for ways to use it to his advantage.

He thought long and hard, turning one idea after another away as impractical. Then he finally settled on one. Walsingham had recently written a poem refuting the ideal that total bliss would result from the totally simple life of two people who eschewed money for a rural life, an opinion that had first been put forward in another's ode. The shoemaker sought out Walsingham's effort and wrote him a letter, praising and quoting it but also mentioning the way he had heard a saying from THE PRINCE quoted, disparaging the monarchy's ways of ruling her subjects as if this locality's rural ways were more important than Her Majesty's chosen religion and the need to keep it pure. He sent the letter knowing that Walsingham, who looked into all things in detail, would find out the name of the place - which he had deliberately omitted - from where it had come. But he had signed the letter.

Walsingham, true to form, did just as he had thought. Then he looked carefully into the circumstances surrounding that writer, asking questions there sending a third party, a trusted but talkative official supposedly checking what taxes were paid locally. He saw the value of the efforts there and came to realize the improper profits and thereby the motives of the venal shoemaker. And Walsingham then talked it all over very quietly with Cecil.

Cecil had ever been very keen on trade. Further he understood that, to create it goodwill was needed. To get such, decent wares at reasonable prices were a necessity. The shoemaker was thereby hoist by his own petard.

He was tried and sentenced to the stocks to be publicly reviled for his greed and further told to repay the money he had taken by deception, putting it into the parish to be used for local alms. Many whose shoes he had made which had failed to be of service turned out gladly to throw rotten food at him.

The pastor, and those on the trading carts, however, did not join in. The shame, they believed, of being in the stocks, together with the way his greed had not eventually profited him at all, was enough. They simply and joyously continued as before, living decently and helping their neighbours with their honesty and diligence.

Back in London, Walsingham and Cecil together toasted their quiet success.

"May all endeavours end so" they said. And Elizabeth continued along the path she firmly believed that God allocated for her to follow. However, 'til having taken her very last breath, although she might worry much about the succession, she adamantly refused to name her heir. Nor would she allow anyone else to do so either. That, she felt, was not only God's prerogative, but also to do so would signal the end of the sovereign's divine right to rule and could lead to a terrible civil war. Elizabeth, right or wrong, loved her country more deeply than that.

Chapter 9

Pre-Reformation, the Vatican, like other royalties and their courts were often more occupied with their own machinations and squabbles; the lower orders were relatively able, on average, to live as they would except they stepped out of the normal line. Post Reformation the Vatican had lessened power with the various countries for all that, still retaining the Vatican States, the Church remained a significant player.

The Vatican's domain covered the major states of Italy from the sixth century until 1861 when the Italian Peninsula was unified by the Kingdom of Piedmont-Sardinia. Reduced, then to the area of Lazio, they continued to exist until 1870. That was the year that, having lost its temporal power to rule often by intrigue or fear, the Vatican took the moral high ground and promulgated the decree that the Pope, speaking *ex cathedra* on matters of faith or morals would be infallible, and that this was to be believed because it was a Papal Decree that had said so. Many disputed this as flawed logic; some theologians openly cited the first near schism within the early church when Peter and Paul disagreed on the necessity for new Christians to accept circumcision to be allowed to join; Paul was shown to be right, Peter fallible. From the 19th Century on, Paul, though still honoured as a saint, had his life and epistles back-pedalled within the Church. True, they were read out in the Masses, but in Latin with the priest's back to the congregation. Most did not clearly hear them and few could construe church Latin at the required speed. Much of the church's distaste for Paul's work had its seed in his letter to the Romans on justification by faith which had the Church feeling side-lined Many doubting theologians, however, did point out that Gregory had chosen Augustine to be the right person to send to convert the English simply because Augustine understood and believed in justification by faith.

One noted theologian was Dollinger, a German theologian, professor of Ecclesiastical History and Law at the University of Munich almost continuously from 1826 to 1871 when he was elected rector. Originally a staunch Ultramontane, he published *Die Reformation* (1846-48) but in 1857 a visit to Rome caused a deep change in his opinions. When the Vatican Council gave the decree of papal infallibility, in March 1871 Dollinger issued a letter withholding his submission. Excommunicated, he took a leading role in calling together a congress at Munich out of which grew the Old Catholics. From then he advocated the union of the various Christian churches in lectures. In two conferences the Anglican and Orthodox churches reached agreements on various points. Dollinger also published a history of moral controversies within the Catholic Church since the 16th Century which seriously questioned how the decree could possibly be true. From the Old Catholics working with the Anglicans, however, the ordination of their vicars could no longer be considered invalid since all, when being ordained, had the hands of an Old Catholic also on the head. No one could still claim that, bishops in England having been appointed by the State, the chain of succession had been broken and their full abilities to function as priests therefore impaired. The church in its teaching, however, air-brushed the Old Catholics out of the picture and said that, apart from the Eastern Churches in schism, she, alone, had 'the Real Presence'.

From then on the Vatican, having lost most of its temporal power at court level, began to meddle more deeply into the everyday lives of ordinary people. They were taught, from childhood, the Vatican was the 'Holy See', that there had never been a disruption in the direct line of succession from Peter, ignoring, of course, the anti-popes when, for fifty years, their line was less than even dotted. To the ten commandments given to Moses, six commandments of the Church were added, one of which told them, under pain of mortal sin, when they must attend a Mass. This was despite the fact that, pre-Reformation in a country under interdict, Mass had been forbidden to be said there.

The Vatican has always had many who would criticize it, people both within the church and outside it. Alexander Pope, born iin 1688 into a Catholic family in England and therefore denied formal education but who had learned much by his reading, had not disowned his faith. However, in one poem he wrote:

Wherever God erects a house for prayer
The Devil always finds a chapel there.
And 'twill be found, upon examination,
The latter hath the larger congregation.[1]

Within the Vatican they were hardly people naïve enough not to know what was factual and what was not; they had been given access to full education. But, true to the Machiavellian principles laid out in THE PRINCE, they not only chose not to disclose anything detrimental to themselves; they actively suppressed it. There were many in the Vatican who had found a new vocation; not so much one of 'feed my sheep' more of herd them around until they are dizzy, fleece them and keep them too poor to buy books. The Beatitude which said, 'Blessed are the meek for they will possess the land' now carried the rider 'if that's all right with the rest of you.' There could even have been some not so politically inclined within Vatican who, like many of those outside, felt called to remain Catholic but who were decent, honest people; they simply did not wish to yield the whole Church to the clutches of the devils.

---

[1] Sometimes attributed to Daniel Defoe but, as they were not contemporaries and Alexander Pope's work has been largely ignored for scorn of his informal schooling, both attributions could be right.

Chapter 10

The first papal decree that was to be considered to be infallible was that the soul of Mary, the mother of Christ, had never known sin from the very moment her own mother had conceived her, that is the doctrine of the Immaculate Conception, that, unlike the rest of mankind, she had never inherited the taint of original sin on her soul.

True to type, Catholic theologians who had doubted papal infallibility fell out over this 'new' doctrine, although it was one many of the laity had held in tradition though not in so many words. Then, in 1858, a young girl, Bernadette Soubirous, claimed to have seen a lady appear to her on a rubbish tip at the Massabielle Rock in Lourdes in the Hautes-Pyrenees. Bernadette was not a stupid child but she was one who had missed most of her schooling as she was a severe asthmatic; complex words or arguments were not in her remit. She came of a good and honest family; her father was a miller making a reasonable living, financially helping many of his neighbours when they were in trouble, her mother was a maternal woman, a natural nurse to whom others who were concerned about a child's health would turn. A prayerful family well-known in the area as being decent, but not famous names generally. Bernadette claimed to have eighteen apparitions of her lady who told her she could not promise her any happiness in this life but only in the next. Bernadette's family sent her to the parish priest for his advice. He said to ask the lady who she was. The answer came back; speaking to Bernadette in the local patois, the lady's reply was, "I am the Immaculate Conception." This meant less than nothing to Bernadette who just did not understand the words but she memorized them to recount to the priest. He was dumbfounded, wondering - among other things - if it were true and, if so, why she had not said "I am the *product* of the Immaculate Conception." Nevertheless, knowing full well both that Bernadette had not thought up the answer herself nor had her family scripted it for her to say, he supported Bernadette's tale and did not just listen to her; he acted throughout as an adviser with her best interests at heart.

As in any small town, word gets around very quickly. She was followed and, during her later visions, she had a growing audience. When, according to her, she was told to dig a hole she grubbed in the earth with her hands. Water started to well up there and, obeying the lady further, she washed her face with the mud. Her onlookers treated her as a figure of fun but the water continued to flow more cleanly than before. It was not long before an ill child declared impossible to heal was cured by that water. The fame of Lourdes then spread. Previously those following and watching Bernadette's every move had been fellow townspeople. Others started to flock in. Their neighbours were fine about this but the magnates in the area were divided. Some saw it as an economic fillip to the town, others thought all these ill people invading will make them all sick. Then there was one particular leader, an avowed atheist, who feared his belief was threatened.

Meanwhile Bernadette's father Francois had his livelihood shattered as were those of all millers when the national laws governing wheat and flours were changed. They had to leave their comfortable home finding various rooms, eventually to be housed in a cell which had been considered too insanitary to use for prisoners. However when the Soubirous family had been so noticeable, Lourdes finally decided to put them in a decent building, better suited to those who had put the town on the map.

Bernadette, older by then, had a boy-friend whom she loved and he loved her. Her dream was to be married as her mother was and, with him to raise a family. Her parents had not only been good people, they had been fine and kind parents, templates which the young couple wished to follow. They were eagerly waiting for their wedding day. But the atheist of the town who had clout was conspiring to have her committed to a mental home; the parish priest told her that her only hope of avoiding this would be to become a nun. Reluctantly and unhappily, she had to go, then, to Nevers to take the veil. Her boyfriend never did marry either.

Throughout her time in Lourdes since the idea that Mary had appeared to her there had been accepted, those making statues had made what they thought would be likenesses of Mary and had shown them to Bernadette who turned her nose up at them. Simpering misses with eyes cast up to the skies struck her as stupid. Though mostly unhappy in Nevers there was a statue at the bottom of the garden there which she preferred; it showed Mary to be filled with motherly concern but by no means in any stupid way. In many respects it would have been closer to something like a photo of Mary; she, who as a newly-pregnant young girl faced the dangers going alone to the hill country of Judea to help her cousin Elizabeth who, as an elderly prima-para, would very probably have an exceedingly difficult delivery. The hills, at that time, were alive with thugs and bandits, runaway slaves who had to steal to survive.

Since Bernadette's time Lourdes has shown the accuracy of Alexander Pope's verse; Mary had asked they should build a church there but people took it further. There was a proliferation of chapels in the domain where many truly devout pilgrims heard Masses but, at some of these, there could be many priests concelebrating. Yet, within five miles, there were churches with no priest for such at all. A care for those parishioners, some of them elderly in harsh hill country, might have been made. The shops outside the domain, too, showed this dichotomy; although there were those with fantastic artwork and one which was a museum of light, there were also many catchpenny places for people with tastes more childish than their pockets, and at least one, just up the hill from the domain, had switchblades and knuckledusters emblazoned with LOURDES for sale in its window. The gimcrack places, too, selling over-priced plastic statues made enough money in six months to retire for the rest of the year. There was no bank to be found nearby but a money-changer who, when there should have been favourable rates, retained higher ones more pleasing to himself. Pilgrims went to Lourdes Monday to Friday; at the weekends there were more murders committed there, in proportion to occupants, than in Paris each year.

However, though Mary appearing in Lourdes will have proved to the faithful the doctrine of the Immaculate Conception, it still did not prove papal infallibility to all. Some even believed, when infallibility is thrown out we should not discard the baby with the bathwater.

To bring Lourdes to the present day floodwaters have inundated the domain; only the Basilica, the church for which Mary had asked, was spared. It may even happen that the devil will have to go looking, in future, for another home.

Chapter 11

The Doctrine of Papal Infallibility, however, had effects that were probably not foreseen, not even by the Vatican politicians, when it was formulated. The need to accept '*the magisterium*' of the church became extended to the clergy and nuns generally; the phrase usually said was 'to respect the cloth'. This allowed those inside that cloth to do just what they would; anybody disputing an action they considered to be bad was simply not to be believed, maybe to be punished for saying 'such a wicked thing'. It was made worse by the age at which boys at that time were taken from their families, to train for the priesthood in a seminary at eleven years old. They may well have felt a calling; whether it was one to take and observe strict vows to serve God by caring for people, or simply to be the big fellow at Masses, back to the congregation, on whom everyone focussed their attention was a moot and largely unaddressed point. The end result was that, though there could be good and holy priests on whom one could depend entirely, there were many fair to middling, but unfortunately too many to whom no one should entrust the care of a wild cat, never mind a child. And nuns took their cues from these priests too.

By and large, also, not only had the beliefs of the Renaissance been forgotten, the generally accepted creed became to be that only Catholics could get to heaven, other Christians, even, please step back. This meant in cold facts that when my grandmother died along with her eighth child in 1904 the eldest, a nine-year-old girl, wanted to go to Mass to pray for the souls of her mother and the baby. Her aunt, a very good and caring woman, one noted for her unusual abilities with children, told the girl probably as gently as she could that it would be pointless as her mother was a non-Catholic and could, therefore, never hope to get to heaven. Further, the souls of un-baptised children were to be stuck in Limbo for all eternity. Yet this was a lady to whom neighbours brought their own children when they had problems, say, a child with any difficulties in speech. The Church's 'teaching' had a strangle-hold on reason but that suited the clerical politicians very well; their main objective being, as ever, for their own advancement and to watch their backs..

Yet, at about the same time there was a Jesuit priest, a curate in a northern town. In his parish the mother of a large brood became seriously ill and had to go to hospital suddenly; her husband was at work at the time down the mine. The priest, hearing her plight, told her not to worry; he'd look after the children who were busy playing then, he'd give them their tea and see to things generally. He sent word to the husband to come home early and heated up the water for his bath; told the fellow to take whatever time he needed to be with his wife, that he would supervise things at home. Then he made the tea and called the bairns in, putting on more water for their baths afterwards. Then, youngest first, he bathed the lot. One of the boys was protesting that he shouldn't be washed. His protests were pooh-poohed and he was dunked like all the rest. Then, pyjama-clad, they said their prayers and went to bed. The priest, whose hobby was embroidery (he had made many of the vestments used in the church) sat down beside the huge basket of socks for darning and, to help the family further, he got to work on them. The next-door neighbour came in later, looking for her son who had been out playing with the rest. That was the unwilling candidate for the bath! As the child was asleep by then, his mother allowed him to stay the night. No one, least of all that priest, had ever asked what religion that neighbour practised.

Then, in the Spring and Summer of 1916, three shepherd children, Lucia Santos and her cousins, Jacinta and Francisco Moto claimed to have been visited by angels on three separate occasions, apparently to prepare them for a later visit. In 1917 on May 13 when they were herding sheep at the Cova da Ina near Fatima they said they saw Our Lady. Lucia described the vision as seeing a woman, 'brighter than the sun, shedding rays of light clearer and stronger than a crystal ball filled with most sparkling water and pierced by the burning rays of the sun'. They ran back to their village to tell everyone what they had witnessed. Further appearances were reported on the 13th of the month in June and July. In these the lady asked the children to pray, make acts of penance in reparation to save sinners, calling for a renewal of care for others. In the course of her appearances she confided three prophesies, known as 'The 3 Secrets of Fatima'. By the first one she said that World War 1 was to end but not before the rise when Communism, an avowed enemy of faith in a deity, should come to rule. She told them it would be hard, then, to be a believer and urged the children to pray especially for Russia. In the second one she predicted an even worse war to follow the first when there had been insufficient good practices whereby the people of the world would pay due regard in their actions for others. The third one was more secret than the two before; to be told only to the Pope who should pass it on to his successor. Others, even within the Vatican, were not to know until the time to make it publicly known to all.

From as early as July 1917 Mary had promised a miracle for the last of her visions on October 13, that all could believe it to be true. What happened then became known as 'The Miracle of the Sun'. A crowd of an estimated 70,000 people , together with journalists and photographers, had amassed at the Cova da Ina. The drizzling rain had finally stopped and a thin layer of cloud shrouded the weak sun. Witnesses later said it could be looked at without hurting the eyes. Lucia, moved she explained by an interior impulse, called out to the people to look at the sun. They looked and saw what they described afterwards as the sun changing colours and spinning like a wheel. What they named as 'the sun's dance' was also seen by others, not in the throng but many miles away. This was fully reported by the columnist Avelino de Almeido in the O SECULO, a very influential paper, pro-government and avowedly anti-clerical. Scientists, doctors and many others climbed aboard the band-wagon, trying to understand how it could happen.

As well as the Miracle of the Sun, the children indicated that a great sign in the night sky would precede a second world war. On January 25 1938 bright lights appeared all over the northern hemisphere, even as far south as North Africa, Bermuda and California, the widest aurora since 1709. Lucia, the sole survivor of the three in '38, wrote letters to her superior and to the bishop the following day saying that this was the sign predicted by Mary. Just over one month later Hitler seized Austria and eight months afterwards he invaded Czechoslovakia.

On August 13 1917 the provincial administrator Artur Santos (no relation of Lucia) believing the events to be disruptive intercepted and jailed the children before they could reach the Cova da Ina that day. Prisoners held there later said the children were consoled by the inmates and then proceeded to lead them in praying the rosary. The administrator, however, threatened them, trying unsuccessfully to get them to tell him the secrets. He told them he would boil them, one by one, in a pot of oil unless they confessed. The children at that time were aged 10, 9 and 7 years old. Unable, then, to see Mary on August 13, she appeared to them on the fifteenth, the feast of the Assumption of Our Lady into Heaven as her last visit to them.

Chapter 12

Different things have been said about what the third secret contained, but all seemed to point to a real shake-up in the Vatican which had been simmering since Angelo Roncalli, the son of a peasant at Sotto il Monte, was elected caretaker-pope in 1958 on the twelfth ballot. Unlike the line of aristocratic Italians before him, he had served as a sergeant in the medical corps and as a chaplain to the troops in World War 1. In 1944 he became the first Papal Nuncio for liberated France and he championed the controversial system of worker priests. Taking the name of John XXII1 caused an uproar in the Vatican. It had been the name of one - and probably the worst - of the anti-popes and it pointed out the lie to the claim of 'unbroken succession'. He convened the 21st ecumenical council to seek unity between the various Christian sects. He also broke with tradition by leaving the Vatican to visit hospitals and prisons in Rome, and, his own sister having lost one of her children at birth, he called the Second Vatican Council. Few truly doubted that the reason for this was to look very carefully at the vexed question of birth control, despite the wishes of those in power who would have preferred to retain the status quo..

As early as October 1951 Pius XII had softened the austere stance of his predecessors on birth control when, in an audience with Italian midwives, he gave permission for Catholics to use the rhythm method when there were serous reasons to avoid procreation. Yet, by the early 60s, it was known to be very fallible, earning the nickname

'Vatican roulette'. At that time a woman who had needed a caesarian section for a safe delivery - a harsher operation in those days - would be advised that, should she become pregnant within two to three years, her womb would be likely to split killing the foetus and probably herself as well, leaving the previous baby to be brought up without a mother. In view of the notorious fallibility of the method allowed, Pope John XXIII set up a Pontifical Commission on the Family in 1962, birth control being one of the major issues it was expected to study. Pope Paul, in his turn, enlarged the Commission until its membership reached 68. The consensus reached (64 votes to 4) by theologians, legal experts, historians, sociologists, doctors, obstreticians and married couples was that a change in the Church's stand was both possible and advisable.

Within the Roman Curia, however, there was widespread reaction to it. So, masterminded by Cardinal Ottoviani, a further report was made. He contacted the four dissenters, the Jesuit Marcellino Zalba, the Redemptorist Jan Visser, the Franciscan Ermenegildo Lio and the American Jesuit John Ford. He persuaded them to enlarge their conclusions in a special report. They even considered, if a womb were agitated when the milk 'came through', that agitation preventing a fertilized egg from implanting, should the mother to be allowed to breast-feed her baby if her husband did not choose to forego their marital life entirely, maybe for nine months. Meanwhile the rest of the Commission, feeling they had done their work and the liberalizing would now commence, having courteously given their findings in, had left to go home.

Throughout '67 and '68, Ottoviani capitalized on the absence of this majority from Rome. Those still within the larger city were exercising great restraint by not putting pressure on the Pope and, by doing so, played right into Ottoviani's hands who marshalled members of the old guard - Cardinals Cicognani, Browne, Parente and Samore - who shared his views and who happened, daily, to meet with the Pope. Every day, then, he was to be told that to approve artificial birth control would be to betray the Church's heritage.

The Church's heritage however had taken something of a beating already by literate lay men and women. Many couples, too, after that 'ruling' found themselves torn, completely unable to go to Mass without feeling like hypocrites or, if able to face the service, barred from Communion. Seeing this huge drop in congregations Cardinal Heenan in England quietly told the priests to remind these people of the old rule of the Church, that if their actions seemed the right things to do according to their consciences for the good of their families there can be no possibility of sinfulness. Unfortunately, bound as he was by his vow of obedience, the laity could not be told directly. Those who had received religious education would know this for themselves but, seeing the damage often being done to the less educated, they were becoming more critical; the airwaves and column inches of the press were jumping with loud voices on the subject. The pointed out the older laws too; that a man marries a woman and the woman marries that man, the priest and the registrar were only there to keep the books straight; that the sacrament of matrimony gives both of them, not through the priests but from each other, graces to help them live their lives well under God; that, as Heenan had reminded the priests, to commit a serious sin it needed three things, grave matter, full knowledge of its evil and total consent of the will to offend God by doing it or no such sin can be committed.

At about that time the Second Vatican Council was publishing its books. Though originally called to address the vexed question of the Church's stance on birth control whenever that question had been raised there papers were waved, the calls of 'Points of Order' had rung out and it had not been allowed. Subsequently it was also air-brushed out of the books. In that part of *GAUDIUM ET SPES* headed The Common Good the words were beautifully comforting but lacked even touching on the most basic details of family life unknown, of course, to any celibate men in the Vatican with little or no experience of pastoral work. Further, recalling the antics of Ottoviani and co, Chapter 27, Respect for the Human Person, rang somewhat hollow at the heart. Generally speaking, when pride should come in the door with love of power or money, virtue and truth can fly out the window. No one can claim to love God thoroughly if unwilling to care for the people He has made, and no one is likely to be looking after others if sincerely concerned, first and foremost, with his or her own welfare. If Vatican City wishes to be known as 'The Holy City' it simply has to get its act together.

Soonest.

The Epilogue

The way the Church's ruling had interfered with marriages and the private lives of Catholics was largely overlooked or, if noted, dismissed by the saying, 'We are a church for sinners'. In the 60s there were more Catholics, per head of population, in prisons, in mental homes, as alcoholics, committing suicide etc. than others. Many young nuns who were prison visitors were horrified by the numbers they found there. When, too, there could be some claiming to be C-of-E because they couldn't spell atheist and didn't know what an agnostic was, the sheer numbers of Catholics outweighing the rest should have given the powers-that-be true pause for thought to ask why is this. But the worst aspect of it was the sheer number of babies damaged or dead because of that ruling.. If a mother has had - as many did have - a non-stop cycle of pregnancy/feeding/pregnancy/feeding for four children or so her blood count and amount of calcium in her body would be low. What mama has, baby can share; no more than that. A foetus, short on nutrients needed for life and healthy growth, cannot climb out of the womb and go shopping for what was essential for survival.

The advice given by at least one priest on the radio at that time to couples was, 'Single beds and be careful what you drink'. So much for Christ's teaching, *Those whom God has joined together let no one put asunder.* Christ's lessons appear not to have carried enough weight then against the ruling of the old guard in the Vatican. Christian charity was not apparent in their remit. In fairness to them, however, it was no more nor less than could be expected from men who were not only celibate, without real, on-going experience of true human love and also who are wedded to power. It can. and usually does erode good sense as it corrupts.

To believe in a good God who has made mankind in his own image and likeness it is necessary also to believe he will, in fact, be on their side. The Old Testament tells us he has carved our names on the palms of his hand. He has care for all people, not just a favoured few.

When in the fourth century there were but a few in northern Africa who were Christians, and when the rest of the Arabs there were hungry for a mono-theistic religion, Jerome once more translated the Bible (the Vulgate) into Latin, ignoring Arabic. So Mohammed, in Arabic Muhammad, was eventually to receive the Koran for them.

The Christian Church, too, has had especially evil times before. In 1209 a young man from the Umbrian region went to see the pope to ask permission to live exactly as Christ had done, in poverty and obedience. As he approached, the pope saw Francis and his eleven companions and had them sent away. But in a dream he saw the Lateran basilica listing dangerously when suddenly a little monk, looking like a beggar, supported it with his shoulder and prevented it from collapsing. The pope then understood that monk had been Francis of Assisi. Francis, however, in resisting the call to write out the recipe for his order of monks appeared to point out that obedience should be given only to God rather than to a collection of clerical lawyers.

Later, when the Church with its monopoly in western Christendom had grown corrupt again, that damage any monopoly can do to humans, Martin Luther was born to challenge it. For God does keep his promises to help in times of danger.

There are many who would say today that, though we hope and work for both ecumenism and inter-faith, that should be for the unity of caring for each other. Humanity seems to do best with plurality, especially if it is flavoured with the understanding of each other's points of view. The Lord/God/Allah/Nature did not make us clones: so why should we believe we must behave as if we were? But we might yet progress to decent lives for all who would have the common good at heart if we would all work hard enough to get it.

God willing.